The Spark Files

Terry Deary trained as an actor before turning to writing full-time. He has many successful fiction and non-fiction children's books to his name, and is rarely out of the bestseller charts.

Barbara Allen trained and worked as a teacher and is now a full-time researcher for the Open University.

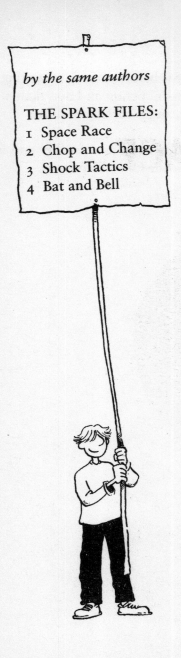

The Spark Files

Book One

SPACE RACE

illustrated by Philip Reeve

faber and faber

First published in 1998
by Faber and Faber Limited
3 Queen Square London WC1N 3AU

Typeset by Faber and Faber Ltd
Printed in England by Mackays of Chatham plc, Chatham, Kent

© Terry Deary and Barbara Allen, 1998
Illustrations © Philip Reeve, 1998

Cover design: Shireen Nathoo

Terry Deary and Barbara Allen are hereby identified as authors
of this work in accordance with Section 77 of the Copyright,
Designs and Patents Act 1988

A CIP record for this book
is available from the British Library

ISBN 0-571-19368-4

10 9 8 7 6 5 4 3 2 1

For my mother, Margaret, with love. BA

BE A SAFE SCIENTIST

IF YOU ARE STRETCHING A RUBBER BAND OR SOMETHING SIMILAR, PROTECT YOUR EYES AND FACE SO THAT IT DOESN'T HURT YOU IF IT SNAPS...

PLATCH

IF YOU ARE DROPPING AN OBJECT FROM A HEIGHT, TAKE CARE IT DOESN'T FALL ON YOU... OR SOMEONE ELSE...

OOPS

10 TONS

NEVER LOOK AT THE SUN DIRECTLY THROUGH A LENS OR COLOURED GLASS. THE LIGHT CAN PERMANENTLY DAMAGE YOUR EYES...

IF THE SUN'S RAYS ARE FOCUSED ON A SMALL AREA -PARTICULARLY THROUGH A LENS- THEY MAY CAUSE BURNING...

NOW THEY TELL ME!

Space Race

File 1

Sam Spark (that's me!)

Handsome hero. Stronger than Superman and cleverer than Sally Spark.

Three cheers for young Sammy
our star
The cleverest young bright Spark
by far

At writing and reading
The class he is leading...
But he's not so good at getting
his poems to
rhyme.

File 2

Sally Spark
  (my slimy sister)

    Face like a prune with glasses
on. Teacher's creepy pet (but
Mum prefers me).

Poor Sally she looks like an ape
Her head is too big for a tape
Though she's top of her classes
Behind those thick glasses
She aint got the brains of
              a grape.

File 3

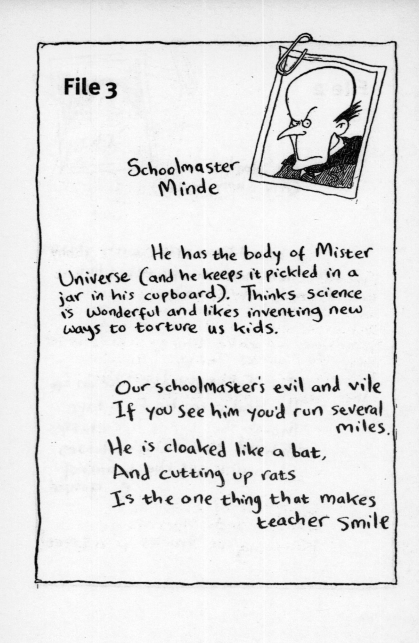

Schoolmaster
Minde

He has the body of Mister
Universe (and he keeps it pickled in a
jar in his cupboard). Thinks science
is wonderful and likes inventing new
ways to torture us kids.

Our schoolmaster's evil and vile
If you see him you'd run several
miles.
He is cloaked like a bat,
And cutting up rats
Is the one thing that makes
teacher smile

File 4

The Spark Family

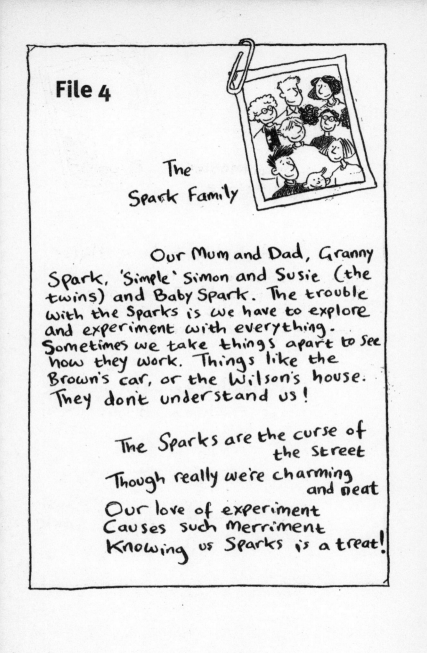

Our Mum and Dad, Granny Spark, 'Simple' Simon and Susie (the twins) and Baby Spark. The trouble with the Sparks is we have to explore and experiment with everything. Sometimes we take things apart to see how they work. Things like the Brown's car, or the Wilson's house. They don't understand us!

The Sparks are the curse of
 the street
Though really we're charming
 and neat
Our love of experiment
Causes such merriment
Knowing us Sparks is a treat!

Chapter 1

It all started last Thursday. Gran was watching the television news at breakfast time. Sister Sally and I were packing our bags ready to go to school.

The news was all about the Russian plan to send two cosmonauts to the Moon . . .

JUST A FEW HOURS TO TAKE-OFF AND THERE IS GREAT EXCITEMENT HERE IN RUSSIA. THE AMERICANS LANDED A MAN ON THE MOON IN 1969, BUT THE RUSSIANS HAVE NEVER MANAGED IT...

Gran shook her head. 'I watched that Moon landing in 1969! I was amazed!'

'Because they landed a man on the Moon?' I asked.

'No! because I always thought the Earth was flat before that! When I were a lass I'm sure the Earth *was* flat!' she said as she sucked on her cornflakes. She'd forgotten to put her teeth in again. 'It looked flat to me.'

Sally put her laptop computer in her school bag and sighed. 'The world is NOT flat, Gran. If it was flat you'd fall off the edge.'

She had a point you know. 'We're doing 'Earth, Moon and Stars' in Science with Master Minde,' I said. 'I think it's because he's an alien.'

Then Sally said, 'I can help you there, little brother. We need to go down to the beach.'

So we said goodbye to Gran and set off for the beach. 'I like the beach,' I said. 'The fairground, the candy-floss stalls, the donkeys.'

'There's only *one* donkey on this beach,' Sally sneered. 'And that's you, Sam! Now, look at that ship sailing away from us,' she ordered. (Did I mention? Sally can be very bossy.)

And, as I watched, it started to disappear. 'Magic!' I said.

Sally said, 'If the sea was flat you'd be able to see that ship for twenty miles.'

'Maybe it just sank!' I gasped. 'Dial 999! Call the coastguard. I've always wanted to dial 999.'

But Sally said, 'Don't be stupid, Sam.'

'I *am* stupid, Sally. You tell me every day,' I reminded her.

'Then try not to *show* it,' she sighed. 'Now, look. Pass me that beach ball.'

'It's not mine,' I told her, 'it belongs to that scruffy little kid.'

I took the kid's ball and passed it to Sally. 'It didn't half hurt,' I groaned.

'He's only a little kid,' she said.

'But his mum's huge!' I said and I mopped the blood from my nose.

Sally took the ball and didn't even say 'Thanks'. Sally's like that.

She said, 'The world is the shape of this big ball. Fetch that little boy's boat and I'll show you what happens when a ship sails over the horizon . . .'

'You fetch it,' I told her.

She came back two minutes later clutching the boat in one hand – and a blood-stained hankie in the other.

I told Sally, 'Of course there's another way to explain the boat disappearing.'

'No there isn't!' she said and her glasses were beginning to steam up. I could tell she was getting angry. I hate making Sally angry. (Not *much* though. Heh! Heh!)

I took a book out of my school bag and showed her.

'Look!' Sally steamed. 'We can set off travelling from here in a straight line. If I am right – if the world is a ball – then we'll end up where we started from. Agreed?'

'So, let's go!' she said.

'I'll be late for school!' I cried. 'Master Minde will be furious!'

'I'll write you a note. I'll say you have to go to the dentist to see about a loose tooth,' Sally promised.

Chapter 2

'I'll pack for the journey. Meet me back at home,' Sally said. (Did I mention that she can be very bossy?)

So I went to school and came face to face with Master Minde. At least I came face to snout with him. He was not very happy when I showed him Sally's note. I can't imagine why!

Dear Bat face
My little brother Sam Spark
wants today off to go to the dentist
to see about his loose tooth. If you
don't believe me then ask him to
waggle it for you.
This note is NOT a forgery and Sam
is NOT skiving off to travel round
the world with his dear and charming sister
Sally.
Signed
(Sam's Mam)

Master Minde poked me with his bat-claw and said, 'We are doing some very important science work today. You will miss it. But don't worry!'

'I *wasn't* worried, sir!' I said.

'I will give you the text book and you can do it all in the dentist's waiting room and finish it off for homework!'

Then he gave me a book called *Suffering Science* and said, 'There is a prize for the best project on the "Earth, Moon and Stars"!'

'What's the prize?' I asked.

'The winner *doesn't* get a detention!' he said and laughed nastily the way he does when he cuts up pickled rats to show us how they work inside. 'And I hope the dentist's drill really grinds through a nerve,' he added.

'Thank you, sir,' I said and went back home.

'Where're you off to?' Gran asked.

'Around the world,' I said.

'Will you be back for tea?' she asked.

'What is it tonight?' Sally asked.

'Pancakes,' Gran told her.

'We'll have to hurry,' Sally told me. 'I like pancakes.'

So we set off down the street and I told her about my homework. 'Don't worry. I'll help you with that,' she promised. 'I've got my computer in my back-pack and all the books we'll need.'

Last time she did my homework I was bottom of the class. She blamed the Maths teacher, Miss Fitt, because old Fatty Fitt just couldn't agree that 2 and 2 makes 22.

I sighed. 'What about lunch?' I asked.

'Chocolate,' she said. I cheered up. It sounded better than the stewed horsemeat in goose-droppings gravy that we got at school dinners.

Sally took out her computer as we walked back to the

seashore. 'Start your homework,' she ordered.

I looked at Master Minde's worksheet. The title was 'Earth, Moon and Stars'.

I took the machine and tapped in the words, 'Earth – Moon – Stars' and asked the machine to search. The first thing it came up with was 'A for Astronomers'. You wouldn't believe what it told me. In fact, I said to Sally, 'You won't believe what this is telling me.'

'I probably would,' Sally sniffed snootily. She looked at the screen . . .

ASTRONOMERS
COPERNICUS 1473-1543

THE CHURCH LEADERS BELIEVED THAT THE EARTH WAS THE CENTRE OF THE UNIVERSE. THEY SAID THE SUN, MOON AND STARS CIRCLED ROUND THE EARTH. BUT A POLISH MONK CALLED COPERNICUS SHOWED THAT THE EARTH WENT ROUND THE SUN AND TURNED. HIS WORK TOOK THIRTY YEARS. HE WAS TOO AFRAID TO WRITE THIS WHILE HE WAS ALIVE BECAUSE THE CHURCH MIGHT HAVE HAD HIM PUNISHED.

'Thirty years!' I cried. 'We can't take thirty years to prove the Earth goes round the Sun. My pancakes'll get cold!'

'Pfutt!' Sally snorted (at least I think that's how you'd spell it). 'I can show you in thirty seconds.'

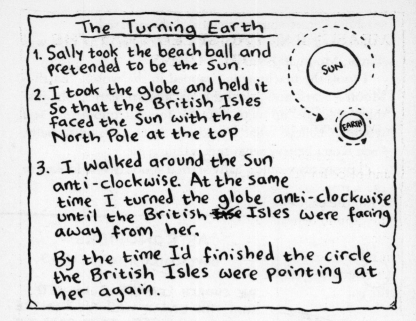

The Turning Earth

1. Sally took the beach ball and pretended to be the Sun.

2. I took the globe and held it so that the British Isles faced the Sun with the North Pole at the top

3. I walked around the Sun anti-clockwise. At the same time I turned the globe anti-clockwise until the British ~~Ise~~ Isles were facing away from her.

By the time I'd finished the circle the British Isles were pointing at her again.

SUN

EARTH

'That's clever, Sally,' I said. It was. You can try this at home if you have a friend to hold the ball.

If you have no friends then use a parent. They just have to stand there and do nothing. Parents are good at that.

'It gets dark when your side turns away from the Sun and light again when it faces the Sun,' Sally said smugly.

'What? Every thirty seconds!' I gasped. I'd have noticed if the Sun went up-down-up every thirty seconds.

'No, dummy,' she said. 'It takes twenty-four hours. Exactly a day.'

'How do you know?' I asked.

'Here. I'll show you,' she said. 'It's all in Master Minde's science book.

MEASURING THE SPEED THAT THE EARTH TURNS

You will need: a magnifying glass, masking tape,
a chair, a piece of white paper,
a watch with a second hand,

1. Tape the handle of the magnifying glass to the chair and place it in the sunlight.

2. Put the paper on the ground beneath the magnifying glass. Move it till the sunlight shines through the glass on to the paper.

3. Move the lens up or down (on a pile of books maybe) till the little circle image of the sunlight is sharp and clear.

4. Draw around that circle very carefully and start timing.

5. Time to see how many seconds it takes for the spot of light to move completely out of the circle.

6. Multiply the answer by 720 and you have the length of the day in seconds. Divide it by 360 to get the number of hours.

'Amazing!' I said. 'The Earth turns every three hundred and eighty-one hours!'

'No. Every twenty-four hours,' Sally said angrily. 'There's something wrong with the second hand of your watch.'

I decided I'd have to take it to a second-hand shop.

'Here, Sally!' I cried. 'Did you know Dad keeps his watch in the bank!'

'Why does Dad keep his watch in the bank?' she asked.

'He's trying to save a bit of time! Heh! Heh!'

Sally didn't laugh. 'Talking of saving time we will go west. We'll follow the Sun. If we go fast enough we will never be in the dark!'

So we started to hurry.

Chapter 3

To the
Seafront

As we walked back to the sea front I looked up the next astronomer . . .

ASTRONOMERS

BRAHE, TYCHO, 1546-1601

SPENT MOST OF HIS LIFE MAKING THE MOST ACCURATE STAR CHARTS OF THE TIME. TYCHO ENJOYED FOOD AND WAS ENORMOUSLY FAT. HE HAD A SHINY METAL NOSE. HIS OWN NOSE HAD BEEN CUT OFF IN A SWORD FIGHT.

IMAGINE THAT! THIS ASTRONOMER HAD NO NOSE!

HOW DID HE SMELL?

TERRIBLE!

We reached the seashore with the sad little donkey and the sadder sunbathers. The sunbathers were sad because the seagulls were using them for target practice. The sea looked flat but I said nothing about that. Instead I said, 'How do we get across the ocean?'

'By boat,' Sally told me. 'The next one leaves at nine o'clock. What time is it now?'

'I don't know. My watch says it's twenty-five past nineteen. I think it's broken.'

'Then we'll have to use the ancient shadow-clock trick!' Sally said. 'Here's one I made yesterday . . .' And she showed me.

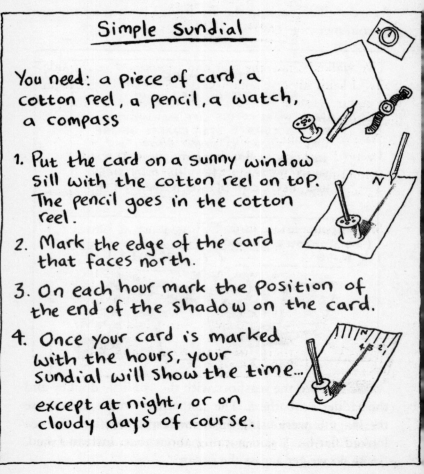

Simple Sundial

You need: a piece of card, a cotton reel, a pencil, a watch, a compass

1. Put the card on a sunny window sill with the cotton reel on top. The pencil goes in the cotton reel.

2. Mark the edge of the card that faces north.

3. On each hour mark the position of the end of the shadow on the card.

4. Once your card is marked with the hours, your sundial will show the time...

except at night, or on cloudy days of course.

'It's nine o'clock now!' I said. There at the end of the pier was a very handy boat. There was a sign that said . . .

ALL ABOARD THE
S.S. TITANIC
PLEASURE CRUISES JUST 50p
PER PERSON
CHILDREN TWO FOR THE PRICE
OF THREE
CAPTAIN: JOLLY ROGER.

We walked along the pier and I looked over the side. 'Sally,' I said, 'there's a man under the pier. He's tied up very tightly with a rope. He's got 'Roger' on the front of his shirt.'

'You're imagining it, stupid,' Sally said.

I waved at the man. 'I'm imagining you!' I cried.

'Mmmmph! Mmmmph! Mmmmph!' he replied.

As we walked along I asked Sally, 'Didn't the *Titanic* sink?'

She tapped a few keys on her computer.

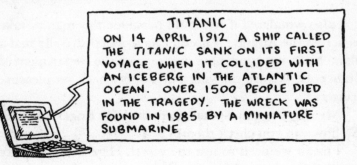

TITANIC
ON 14 APRIL 1912 A SHIP CALLED
THE *TITANIC* SANK ON ITS FIRST
VOYAGE WHEN IT COLLIDED WITH
AN ICEBERG IN THE ATLANTIC
OCEAN. OVER 1500 PEOPLE DIED
IN THE TRAGEDY. THE WRECK WAS
FOUND IN 1985 BY A MINIATURE
SUBMARINE

'Sally!' I squawked. 'The *Titanic* is a wreck!'

'Not *this* one. This one is probably just named after the great ship.'

'But it's an *unlucky* name.'

'Don't be stupid.'

'The *Titanic* sank!'

'Only *once*!' she argued. 'Now get on board!'

The man at the end of the gangplank was dressed like a pirate and was as ugly as old Master Minde!

I also wondered if we could persuade this man to take us across the Atlantic. I needn't have worried. Sally had a plan. 'Now, my good man, we are from the Department of Transport. We are carrying out a spot check on pleasure cruisers.'

'My ship's got no spots!' Captain Jolly Roger laughed. 'So how can you check them?'

'I mean we need to test the vessel. Here is my identity card!' Sally showed him her bus pass . . . very quickly. 'Now get off the ship at once and we'll sail it away.'

'Aharrrrh! Sal, lass!' he cackled and hobbled off the ship on his crutches.

'There's something odd about that man,' I thought as Sally connected her computer to the ship's engines.

'This will give maximum performance,' she said as she switched on and we shot over the water. The flags were the first things to be blown away. Then bits began to drop off the ship.

'What if we hit an iceberg?' I asked above the roaring sound of rushing water.

'It had just better get out of my way!' Sally laughed. 'But it's your job to set us a course.'

'I can't do that!' I said.

'You learned to read a compass when you were in the Cubs didn't you? Before you were thrown out for cheating on your knot test?' (It was true. I used super glue. It took Akela weeks to separate herself from my granny knot.)

'I can't read the compass because I am being very seasick!' I said. To prove it I kept a bit of my sick in my journal. Here it is . . .

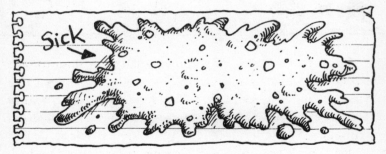

'Oh, I'll do it,' Sally snapped and she stepped up on to the ship's bridge. Then she gave a scream. She pointed at the control panel. 'The compass!'

I hurried up the steps and stood beside her, 'The compass!' I cried.

There it was . . .

Adrift in a cruel and pitiless sea without a compass to guide us.

Chapter 4

'Where can it be?' Sally groaned.

'I think I know!' I said quietly. I remembered Captain Jolly Roger ...

'He wants us to get lost!' I said. 'It's all part of some cunning plan.'

'His cunning plan won't work!' Sally said grimly.

'Yes it will!' I cried. 'We are in the middle of an empty ocean with no compass. We haven't got a chance.'

'You're forgetting I trained with the Brownies . . . before I was thrown out for cheating in the cookery test.' (Sally had put sheep's eyes in a food processor to make eyes-cream. It took Brown Owl weeks to stop having the nightmares.) 'Here's my Brownie Manual. It tells you how to make your own compass!'

Make a Compass

You need: a magnet, a sewing needle, a saucer, tape, cork, and paper.

1 Cut out a disc of paper so that it fits comfortably on the edge of the saucer. Mark it with the points of the compass, N, S, E, and W.

2 Stroke the needle 10–12 times with the south pole of a magnet (from the eye of the needle to the point). You must stroke in the same direction each time.

3 Tape the magnetized needle to a slice of cork. Put some water in the saucer and float the cork on top.

4 The point of the needle will point north. Turn the paper disc so that North lines up with the point of your needle.

You have made a compass.

With the help of the compass we sailed west ahead of the Sun. The Sun said it was nine o'clock now but my stomach said it was dinner time.

'We're not going fast enough,' Sally said. 'The trouble with sailing west is you're sailing into the wind most of the time. The Vikings had this problem when they discovered America.'

'Hah! Smarty pants!' I cried. 'Christopher Columbus discovered America, not the Vikings. Everyone knows that.'

'Eric the Red landed in North America a thousand years before Columbus,' Sally said. 'I thought everyone knew that!'

She was so smug you could just poke her in the eye. We shared the chocolate and the Sun still said it was morning but the ship's clock said it was afternoon. 'We'll have to change the ship's clock,' Sally said as we sighted the coast of Canada.

'Take it back to the shop, you mean? Change it for a new one? It's a long way.'

'No, I mean change the time. Here they are four hours behind us in England. And it took us four hours to cross the Atlantic. So we've arrived at the same time we set off!'

She showed me the globe . . .

WE USED A GLOBE, BUT YOU COULD USE A BALL WITH "X" TO MARK YOUR COUNTRY...

1. SALLY HELD THE GLOBE. I SHONE A TORCH ON IT AS SALLY TURNED IT SLOWLY ANTI-CLOCKWISE. THE TORCH IS THE SUN.

2. WHEN THE SUN IS DIRECTLY OVER YOUR COUNTRY IT IS NOON. THE COUNTRIES TO MY LEFT (THE WEST) ARE STILL WAITING FOR NOON, SO IT MUST BE MORNING. THEY ARE "BEHIND" OUR COUNTRY.

← WEST   EAST →

3. PUT A TRAINED BEETLE ON THE SPOT MARKED X. THEN ASK IT TO WALK 'WEST' AS THE GLOBE TURNS ANTI-CLOCKWISE. IF IT TRAVELS AT THE SAME SPEED AS THE EARTH IS TURNING IT WILL ALWAYS BE NOON

IF YOU DON'T HAVE A BEETLE, LET YOUR FINGERS DO THE WALKING.

That's what we'd done! Set off at nine in the morning and arrived at nine in the morning! Just in time for breakfast.

An Inuit was just having a fry-up on the ice as we crashed the *Titanic* on to the shore of Northern Canada and jumped ashore with Sally's computer and back-pack.

'We're too far north,' Sally said with a frown. 'The compass must have been a bit off. There must have been some magnet on the ship pulling it off line. I wonder where it was?'

I felt the magnet in my trouser pocket and said nothing. Anyway, I'd always wanted to meet an Inuit.

'Good morning!' the Inuit said. 'Have some breakfast.'

I sniffed at the mess in the frying pan. 'What is it?' I asked.

'We eat whale meat and blubber,' he said.

'If I ate whale meat I'd blubber too!' I told him. 'I'll stick to chocolate.'

'Do you have an ig-loo?' Sally asked suddenly.

'Yes? Why?'

'Because I need an ig-pee,' she said. 'I'm bursting!'

The man pointed to an ice house with a wooden door. There was a door marked 'Ice Maidens' and she hurried inside.

The man in the furry suit dipped a leather bucket into the hole in the ice and filled it with freezing water. Then he walked up to the door of the loo and threw the water over. It quickly froze and turned to glittering crystals in the morning sun.

'Why did you do that?' I asked.

'The door is frozen shut now! Your sister will never get out!' Suddenly he let the hood drop and I saw the evil face of the man who called himself Jolly Roger – though he looked more like Master Minde in disguise. 'Hah! Foiled you this time! You will *never* get out in time to hand your project in! You could spend the rest of your life in detention!'

He took a small controller out of his pocket and pressed some buttons. The tower of a small yellow submarine appeared in the hole in the ice. He opened the lid, jumped in and waved. 'You think you're Bright Sparks!' he jeered. 'My dog's got more bright barks than you! Hee! Hee!' he laughed and slammed the lid after him.

The submarine slid below the surface and left me alone with a pan of blubber and a sledge. I knew that if I became truly desperate and was absolutely starving I might just manage to eat that sledge. Sally was hammering at the door. 'It's jammed!' she wailed with a chilling cry – a sort of ice scream. 'Get me out, Sam!'

'I can't!' I said. 'Our evil enemy has frozen the door shut and I haven't got a blow torch to unfreeze you.'

'Ahhhh! Then I'm doomed to die in this frozen waste! What a waste!'

I could see our gravestone now . . .

Here lies clever Sally Spark
Here lies brother Sammy too
Gone to heaven with the Angels
Frozen in an igloo loo

Chapter 5

'I am doomed, Sam, doomed,' Sally sighed. 'But I will be brave to the end. I want you to take that dog-sled and save yourself, Sammy. Save your precious little life.'

'OK, Sal! Cheerio!' I said.

'Get back here you miserable little worm!' she screamed loud enough to frighten the whales beneath the ice. 'You are *supposed* to say you will never desert me.'

'*You will never desert me.* There you are. I've said it. Can I go now? My toes are getting cold.'

'When I get out of here I will find the biggest piece of ice I can lift and stuff it down the back of your miserable little neck,' she threatened.

'Ah, but you can't get out, Sally. I don't have anything to unfreeze the door,' I reminded her. Anyway, I didn't really want ice down the back of my neck.

'Of course you can set me free. The Sun sends more heat to Earth every second than all of our power stations make in a *year*! Did you know that?'

'No, but I'll bet you are going to tell me,' I muttered.

'You have the magnifying glass and you have the science book. Get me out of here!'

So I opened the science book. I opened it at a page that said . . .

The Death Ray

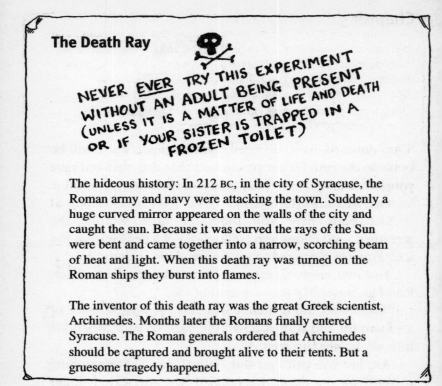

NEVER _EVER_ TRY THIS EXPERIMENT WITHOUT AN ADULT BEING PRESENT (UNLESS IT IS A MATTER OF LIFE AND DEATH OR IF YOUR SISTER IS TRAPPED IN A FROZEN TOILET)

The hideous history: In 212 BC, in the city of Syracuse, the Roman army and navy were attacking the town. Suddenly a huge curved mirror appeared on the walls of the city and caught the sun. Because it was curved the rays of the Sun were bent and came together into a narrow, scorching beam of heat and light. When this death ray was turned on the Roman ships they burst into flames.

The inventor of this death ray was the great Greek scientist, Archimedes. Months later the Romans finally entered Syracuse. The Roman generals ordered that Archimedes should be captured and brought alive to their tents. But a gruesome tragedy happened.

'What are you doing out there, Samuel?' my sister asked politely.

'Reading a story about a gruesome tragedy,' I said. I almost lost my place.

'There will be just one gruesome tragedy around here and that will be when I get my hands on you! Get me out of here _now_!'

'Just a minute . . .'

'NOW!'

'I'm just looking for the magnifying glass,' I lied as I read on.

A soldier burst into the room where Archimedes was working. The old man was scratching a plan on the floor and told the soldier not to disturb him. The soldier drew his sword and ordered the scientist to stop scratching on the floor or he would kill him. Archimedes ignored him. This made the soldier so furious he brought his sword crashing down on the old man's skull. The world's greatest brains lay spattered over the dust of the floor.

'I am going to count to ten and then I am going to get really, *really* angry!' Sally was screeching. I wished a Roman soldier with a sword could have come along at that moment. I turned the page . . .

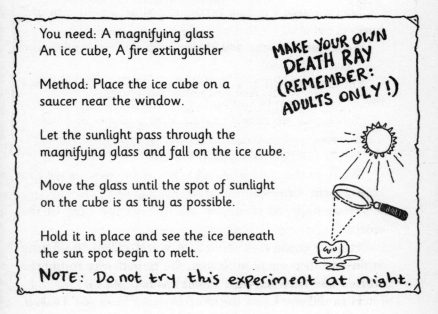

You need: A magnifying glass
An ice cube, A fire extinguisher

MAKE YOUR OWN DEATH RAY (REMEMBER: ADULTS ONLY!)

Method: Place the ice cube on a saucer near the window.

Let the sunlight pass through the magnifying glass and fall on the ice cube.

Move the glass until the spot of sunlight on the cube is as tiny as possible.

Hold it in place and see the ice beneath the sun spot begin to melt.

NOTE: Do not try this experiment at night.

I quite liked the idea of Sally's toilet door bursting into flames. But she had the chocolate with her so I decided it would not be a good idea. Instead I pointed the death ray at the ice around the door and melted it steadily. After an hour she was free. Red-faced, furious and with steamed-up glasses . . . but free.

I nipped into the igloo loo next door to Sally's 'Ice Maidens' door. It said 'Snow Men'. I thought I saw a fat old feller with a long white beard on the floor. He had a red suit under the tight ropes that bound him and the dirty sock that gagged his mouth. Yeuch!

'Nnnng! Nnnng! Nnnng!' he said.

'Sorry, fatso, I'm just imagining you!' I told him and hurried outside.

We leapt on to the dog sledge with our equipment and Sally cried, 'Mush!'

The dogs set off at a furious pace. And we hissed over the frozen wastes of Canada.

'Where are we now?' I asked after a couple of hours.

'Alaska.'

'You'll ask her? Ask who?' I asked her.

'We're in the state of Alaska. It's as far west as we can go in North America.'

'What happens then? Do we fall off the edge of the world?'

'No, we come to a stretch of water called the Bering Strait and then we're in Russia. We're half-way round the world!' she cried happily. 'Mush! Mush! Mush!'

'How did you know the word to make them go?' I asked.

Sally looked smug. 'Because I'm a genius,' she said. 'I know practically everything.'

'So what word do you use to make them stop, Sally?' I asked.

She turned a little pale. 'Err . . . err . . . err . . .'

I tried that on the huskies. 'Err . . . err . . . err!' I cried. Nothing happened. 'Nothing happened, Sally,' I told her.

'Err . . . oh, dear,' she said as she saw the Pacific Ocean racing towards us.

AAAAAAAAAAAAARGH!

Chapter 6

'We've just flattened a penguin!' I cried over the rushing wind.

'There are *no* penguins in the Arctic – penguins only live in the Antarctic,' know-all Sally told me.

'Oops! Then we've just flattened a nun!'

'These dogs are so fast!' Sally cried. 'They're just not human!'

'They're not even very doggy. I've never seen dogs with antlers,' I told her as we rushed towards the end of the land and a very high cliff.

'Reindeer! That's what they are! Reindeer! They're not huskies, stupid!' she laughed. The cliff was a few metres away. I don't know what she had to laugh about.

'Like Father Christmas,' I nodded as the animals leapt off the edge of the cliff. I waited for the sick feeling you get when a lift drops suddenly. It never came. 'We're flying!'

Sure enough we soared over the islands and the ships below, still heading west.

'I guess the old guy tied up in the "Snow Men" loo was Father Christmas!' I said. 'We've got his sleigh.'

'There's no such person as Father Christmas,' Sally told me. 'You imagined him.'

I looked at the wild and freezing water a mile below us. I hoped I wasn't imagining the sleigh too. We drifted down towards the coast and Sally looked pleased. She showed me a map. 'We're here,' she said, pointing. (I have to say the Earth looked pretty flat to me on this map.)

I jabbed a finger at a line on it and asked, 'What does that line mean?'

WHAT DOES THAT LINE MEAN?

Sally told me, 'That's the International Date Line. You go back in time as you travel west and forward when you travel east. When you reach the date line you go forward a day when you're travelling west, and back a day when you're travelling east.'

'But we're travelling west.'

'Right, my bright and sparky brother,' she grinned.

'So, if we left on Monday morning we've just crossed into Tuesday. We're already a day late!'

Sally's grin slid from her face like jelly off a greasy plate. She grabbed me by the throat and shook me hard. 'You're right! I got it wrong! We should have gone east! Nyaaaagh! Why did you let me do that, you stupid Spark! At this rate we'll get back on Tuesday instead of Monday! It's all your fault!' she screamed.

'I thought it might be.'

'So what are you going to do about it?' she demanded.

'I'll do my project as we travel, I suppose. If we arrive at nine on Tuesday morning I'll go straight to school. I need to write something about the Moon and the planets and the project's finished. What do you know about the Moon, Sally?'

She scowled. 'It's made of green cheese,' she muttered. She was definitely in a sulk.

'No it's not!' I said, excited. 'It's made of rock! If I put a sample of Moon rock in my project I'm bound to get top marks.'

'Even this sleigh won't go to the Moon,' she snapped.

'No, but a rocket will,' I said and pointed across the plains to where a huge rocket pointed towards the sky.

Even Sally brightened at the sight. 'The Russian Space Base. It might just work! Whoa!' she cried and the reindeer slowed to a halt.

We jumped down and landed with a squelch in some mud. 'What's this?' I asked.

'Mush,' Sally explained.

No sooner had she said the word than the reindeer galloped off and left us alone at the station. Oh, well, we'd have to find another way to get back home. We walked towards the great gates. 'I hope it's a full moon when we get there.'

'Why's that?'

'We'll never be able to land on the skinny bit if it's a new moon.'

Sally scowled at me. 'The Moon doesn't get bigger or smaller. It's just the bit that's lit up that changes. Look . . . here's an experiment to explain it . . .'

Chapter 2 HITTING THE MOON

If you have reached Chapter 2 then you didn't blow up on take-off. Now you are probably worried about hitting the Moon. Do not worry. The Moon does not go away. Here is how you can prove it and speed happily through space: You will need a desk lamp, an old tennis ball, a pencil and a pen.

Stick the pencil through the tennis ball. Use the pen to mark a small cross on the side of the ball.

Switch on the lamp and darken the room. Hold the tennis ball at arm's length with the spot towards you. The ball is the Moon. You are the Earth.

Spin slowly on the spot, keeping the ball in front of you with the cross always facing you. You'll see how the lit part of the Moon changes from a thin curve to a full circle as you spin round. And the Earth always sees the same face of the Moon (with the cross in the middle) and never the back of the Moon.

'See?' Sally said. 'No problem.'

'Just the problem of getting on to the spaceship.'

'Leave it to me.' She walked up to the door of the spaceship. An old man with wild white hair like a demented dandelion was standing there with a book called *Rocket Journeys for Beginners*.

'I'm from the British Ministry of Interplanetary travel. We've come to do a spot check on your ship!'

'My ship's got no spots so how can you check them?' the man asked and he cackled. There was something familiar about that face, that cackle and that joke. I should have known better than to follow Sally on board.

We put on spacesuits and settled in the cabin. There was a television screen in front of us and a lever.

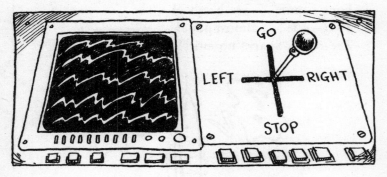

Suddenly the television screen showed us mission control. I wondered why all the controllers had ropes tying them to their chairs and gags in their mouths.

The white-haired professor's face appeared. He was grinning nastily. 'Sorry, you didn't have a return ticket!' he laughed.

There was no point in saying anything to Sally. I knew she'd say I was imagining it. Then the voice crackled through the speakers.

'Five – alive . . . but not for long . . .

Four – three . . . tee-hee-hee!

Two – one . . . almost gone!

Zee-ro . . . Sparks no more!'

Chapter 7

'Cor, Sal, this is incredible. Look at those people down there. They're so small they look like ants.'

'They are ants you idiot, we haven't taken off yet.'

'Arrrrgghh,' I groaned as my stomach yo-yoed between my mouth and my feet. I thought that it was lucky I'd been sick earlier because it would have been a lot messier in a spacesuit.

'Are we nearly there yet?' I asked. Sally glared at me (just like dad does in the car). 'I spy with my little eye something beginning with S,' I said.

'Just do some work on your project. Here's my computer.'

I typed the words *space* and *travel* into the computer.

> ROCKETS WERE PROBABLY INVENTED BY THE CHINESE ABOUT 700 YEARS AGO. THEY WERE USED AS FIREWORKS AND SOMETIMES AS WEAPONS IN BATTLES. IN 1903 A RUSSIAN SCHOOL TEACHER CALLED KONSTANTIN TSLOLKOVSKY DESIGNED A SPACESHIP. HIS IDEA WAS TO POWER IT WITH LIQUID OXYGEN AND LIQUID HYDROGEN... EVERYONE THOUGHT HE WAS MAD.

'What if he *was* mad, Sally? *Our* teacher's mad. What if space travel *isn't* possible? What if we are imagining all this?' I was beginning to hope that I was imagining it or dreaming it. I couldn't even pinch myself to see if I was dreaming.

'Calm down you idiot and get on with your work. I'm busy,' Sally said. She was frowning at a load of dials and flashing lights.

AMERICANS WHO GO INTO SPACE ARE CALLED ASTRONAUTS BUT RUSSIANS ARE CALLED COSMONAUTS.

'But I'm British. What am I called, Sally?'

'Sam.'

Sometimes I don't think Sally listens to me. I could see the Earth through the tiny window in the space rocket. It looked just like the pictures I'd seen at school. It's just a green and blue disc.

'My stomach says it's tea-time,' I said.

'Your stomach always says it's tea-time. It should be safe to take your helmet off.'

I took my helmet off. 'Why haven't you taken your helmet off, Sally?'

'I just wanted to make sure it was safe,' she smiled.

'I could have died?'

'It could have been worse. It could be *me* that died.'

Sally passed me some chocolate and I put it on the control panel in front of me while I took my gloves off. I didn't want chocolate on my gloves. It's not that I mind getting my gloves chocolatey it's just that it's easier to lick off your fingers. But when I looked back, my chocolate had gone.

'Sally, give it to me. Give me my chocolate.'

'Have you eaten it already?'

'No. I put it down and now it's gone. So you must have nicked it.'

'How do you know it was me?'

'We're the only two people here.'

'I haven't got it. Are you sure we're the only people here?'

'Y – e – s. I think so. I hope so.'

Sally was just trying to scare me. She was also succeeding. I was beginning to think that school was a really nice place to be. I would be safe in school – apart from when the school bully got me in a corner . . . but the French teacher is like that with everyone.

Sally's eyes widened behind her glasses. 'Look behind you,' she said seriously.

'I don't want to.' I'd seen all those old films. The hero looks behind him and there's some horrible alien going to splatter him all over the spaceship. I didn't want to be splattered. I didn't feel hungry any more.

'Look behind you,' Sally said again, 'and you'll get a surprise.'

'That's what I'm afraid of!'

I turned slowly and there it was . . .!!!

'Wow, now that's really clever. How did you do that, Sally?'

'It's not me, that's what happens in space. If you weren't strapped in then you'd be floating around as well.'

Sally passed me a page from the science book. 'Read this while I try and work out what this computer's doing,' she said.

Isaac Newton is one of the most famous scientists in the world. He studied science and mathematics at Cambridge University. In 1666 the plague reached Cambridge and the University was closed. Newton went to stay at his mother's farm in Lincolnshire. One day he was sitting in the orchard and watched an apple fall to the ground because of the pull of gravity. He wondered if gravity was keeping the moon in orbit around the Earth. And if this was how the planets stayed in orbit around the Sun. It was twenty years before he found the answer.

Sally said, 'Some books say that the apple fell on his head.'

'Well that would explain why it took him twenty years to find the answer. The bang on the head probably made old Isaac forget what he was doing,' I said.

'In space the pull of gravity is less than it is on Earth. On the Moon you can jump six times higher than on Earth,' Sally said. 'And when you are in space you are weightless. Look, here's an experiment I had to try for homework.' She fished a worksheet out of her back-pack.

YOU COULD TRY IT NOW AND LET US KNOW WHAT HAPPENS...

Weightlessness

You will need:
bathroom scales, a heavy book or brick, a bed.
1. Put the book (or brick) on the
scales and weigh it. Write
down the weight.
2. Now hold the scales
(with the book on it)
just above a soft bed.
(Make sure no one's in the bed)

3. Drop the scales on to the bed and
watch the reading drop below zero as
the scales fall. This is because the
book has become weightless.
It weighs the same once it lands
on the bed again.

'So the book hasn't changed in size – it just weighs less,'
I said.

'Look, we're getting close to the Moon. It's time to get
ready for landing,' Sally said bossily.

I grabbed the rest of the chocolate and stuffed it in my
mouth. We put our helmets back on. I thought of what it
must have been like for those first men who landed on the
Moon. I was about to find out. As we got closer we could
see that the Moon was covered with craters and boulders.
It looked just like next door's back garden to me.

Suddenly the lights on the control panel started to flash and the rocket changed course. The screen of the onboard computer flickered on. I could see the shadowy outline of the white-haired Russian scientist. The look on his face made my stomach churn. As I saw him press a series of buttons, I heard him cackle, 'There'll be no small steps for Sam Spark. Just a giant leap into the unknown!'

I felt the rocket change course. It was a course that took us away from the Moon. And off into space.

Chapter 8

'Where are we going, Sally?' I asked my sister.

'We are boldly going where no boy, girl, monkey or dog has ever boldly gone before. We are going past the Moon and on to the planets! Boldly,' she said.

'I don't feel very bold,' I told her.

The Moon was shrinking very fast behind us. I turned and looked out of the window to my right. A dusty red ball rushed past. 'What was that?' I squawked.

'Mars, I think,' Sally said and punched the words *solar system* into her computer.

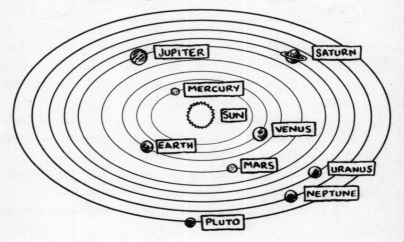

THE SOLAR SYSTEM IS THE SUN AND ALL THE BODIES THAT ORBIT AROUND IT – NINE PLANETS AND THEIR MOONS AS WELL AS COMETS AND ASTEROIDS. THE NINE PLANETS OF OUR SUN ARE (IN ORDER) MERCURY, VENUS, EARTH, MARS, JUPITER, SATURN, URANUS, NEPTUNE AND PLUTO.

The evil controller's face grinned at us from the screen. 'Well, my little friends, it looks like the end for you. Unless, of course, you can answer this simple riddle.'

Sally squinted through her glasses at the screen. 'I'm good at riddles. What's the prize?'

'If you answer the riddle then I will make sure you land safely!' the man cackled.

'Go ahead,' Sally said. (I could see her fingers hovering over the keys of her computer. She was going to get the machine to solve the riddle. That's cheating!)

'There are nine planets orbiting the Sun. Which is the odd one out?' the man said and his grin was like a Rottweiler when it sees a burglar's leg. 'I'll call back in five minutes! If you're right, you get to land. If you're wrong you rocket off into outer space and you'll never get that project handed in on time! Heh! Heh!'

The screen went blank. Sally was already tapping furiously at the keys. After a minute the computer whirred and crackled and the screen flashed.

Sally stared at the screen and turned pale. 'It's let me down,' she whispered. 'The computer's let me down!'

I'll swear there were tears behind those big glasses of hers.

WHAT SORT OF QUESTION IS
THAT? I AM NOT PROGRAMMED
FOR RIDDLES. EVERY PLANET
IS THE ODD ONE OUT FOR ONE
REASON OR ANOTHER. MY GOD!
YOU HUMANS HAVE SOME STUPID
GAMES. WELL, I'M NOT PLAYING
THIS ONE OR I'LL BURN OUT MY
INTEGRATED PROCESSOR!

She stared at the message over and over again. I stared at it and smiled. 'My *God*!' I said. 'That's the clue!'

Sally shook her head. 'We're doomed to spend the rest of our lives in this tiny capsule. Imagine it! The rest of my life . . . with *you*!'

She could hurt somebody's feelings, that girl. Luckily I don't have any. The screen on the control panel lit up again and that ugly face leered out at us. 'Well, Bright Spark? What's the answer?'

'I . . . I . . . don't . . .' Sally began.

'The answer,' I cut in, 'is that Earth is the odd one out. All of the other planets are named after Greek or Roman gods!'

Sally turned slowly and looked at me. 'That's right! Mercury's the Roman messenger god and Venus is the Roman god of love!'

'Mars is the god of chocolate bars and Pluto's the god of cartoon dogs!' I guessed. (We'd done 'Gods' with Miss Fitt last term so I knew the answer.)

'Grrrr!' the scientist growled.

'Grrrr . . . eat!' Sally cried and hugged me.

'So now you have to keep your promise! Let us land safely!'

His cruel eyes sparkled like slime on a frog's back. 'You land in ten minutes,' he promised.

'We're more than ten minutes from Earth,' Sally argued.

'I didn't say anything about *Earth*!' he growled. 'You land in ten minutes on Pluto!'

A small ball of ice appeared in front of the spaceship. 'Pluto!' Sally cried. 'We're finished!'

'We can land and fly home again, can't we?' I asked.

'We have enough fuel for one blast of the rockets. We can use it to slow us down . . . but then we'll not have enough to take off again.'

'What'll happen if we don't slow down?' I asked.

Sally peered at me through her glasses. 'We'll hit Pluto like a meteorite hits the Moon. You've seen the craters on the Moon, haven't you? Read Professor Birdbrain's book on craters to see how they're made!'

I turned to the book and opened it at the page marked . . .

Meteorite Craters

Even someone as stupid as you can make your own meteorite crater with this simple experiment. You need a baking tray, a packet of plain fine flour, a ruler and a spoon. For weedy little kids like you you'll also need a chair and lots of newspaper for the floor because this is extremely messy! Cover the bottom of your tray with the flour till it is about 2 cm thick. Smooth the top of the flour with the ruler. This is what the Moon looked like when it was first formed. Now place the tray on the newspaper on the floor. Climb on your chair with a small spoonful of flour. Hold it about 2 metres above the tray. Let the flour drop.

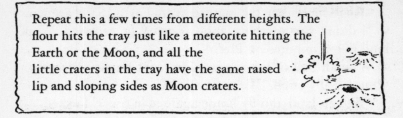

Repeat this a few times from different heights. The flour hits the tray just like a meteorite hitting the Earth or the Moon, and all the little craters in the tray have the same raised lip and sloping sides as Moon craters.

'We're like the blobs of flour about to hit the tray,' Sally said. 'Pow! The greatest meteorite crater on Earth is in the Arizona Desert. It made a hole 1265 metres wide and 175 metres deep!'

'Fire the rockets and save us!' I cried. 'I don't want to end up 1265 metres wide!'

Sally fired the rockets and used up the last of our fuel. We floated down to the surface of Pluto like a feather.

Chapter 9

'We've boldly gone and done it now,' I said, looking out on to the frozen rocks of the tiny planet. 'Let's explore and collect some rock. I always take Granny a stick of rock when I go on my holidays.'

The planet was so small it had hardly any gravity. I broke the Olympic long jump, high jump and pole-vault records with my first step.

I was just starting to enjoy myself when I saw it. Whoosh! A bright white light passed across the sky leaving a faint tail. No sooner had it vanished than a ball seemed to bobble across the frozen surface. As it got nearer I saw the ball in fact had about fifty legs all over its surface. Each leg ended in a boot and the boots were rolling it towards me like a runaway football. A face on the front of the ball saw me and it screeched to a halt. The face looked terrified.

'What's that, Sally?' I asked.

'It's an alien,' she said. 'And it looks terrified to me. Have you been pulling one of your stupid faces at it?'

'No, Sally. It's trying to speak!'

Sure enough the mouth in the face was moving. 'Aliens!' it said.

'No, we're just a couple of kids from the planet Earth! *You're* the alien!'

'Look, if *I* come to Earth *I'm* an alien. But since *you've* come to Pluto that makes *you* the aliens. OK?'

'Fine,' I shrugged and we introduced ourselves.

'Hi, Sally and Sam,' the Plutonian said. 'I'm Bruto from Pluto just off to find a shelter from the Sun Dragons,' he said.

'What dragons? You have dragons on Pluto?' I asked.

'Yeah! You just saw one flashing across the sky. We Plutonians are terrified of them! The others are all hiding in the shelters. I was caught out playing balloon racing.'

I noticed that Sally wasn't taking any notice and seemed to be playing with her computer. 'Sally, I don't think now is the time to be playing computer games,' I told her.

'I'm not playing games, you idiot, I'm looking something up. Got it. Look at this.' She showed me and the alien the screen.

COMETS

A COMET IS JUST A HARMLESS BALL OF ICE AND DUST. USUALLY THEY ARE INVISIBLE BUT, AS THEY APPROACH THE SUN, THE HEAT MAKES THE CORE MELT. A CLOUD OF GAS AND DUST IS RELEASED AND CATCHES THE LIGHT

IN PAST TIMES PEOPLE BELIEVED COMETS WERE SIGNS FROM HEAVEN THAT A DISASTER WAS ABOUT TO HAPPEN. SOME PRIMITIVE PEOPLE, LIKE THE ANCIENT CHINESE, EVEN BELIEVED THAT COMETS WERE DRAGONS AND THE COMET'S TAIL WAS FIRE. THEY ARE NOT. COMETS ARE HARMLESS

'You see – it's not a Sun Dragon, it's just a comet,' she said.

The alien gave a wide grin. 'Your knowledge has slain the Dragons of Pluto! How can I ever repay you?'

'You can give us enough rocket fuel to get us off Pluto!' I said.

'Sorry, we don't have rocket fuel. But Pluto has so little gravity it would only take a sharp blast to get you off,' Bruto said. 'Why, sometimes we lose our balloons if we blast them off too fast. Here, I'll show you.'

I took out my space pen and space paper and sketched Bruto's racing balloon . . .

Balloon Rockets

You need:
Two paper clips, sticky tape, a balloon
strong thread, two chairs.

1. Open the paper clips up so there
is a straight piece that can be taped to
the balloon at each end.

2. Blow up the balloon, seal
the end with tape and stick
the hooks on top.

3. Fasten one end of the thread to a
chair, stretch it across and fasten the
other end to a second chair

4. Hook the balloon onto the tight
line. Take the tape off the end of the
balloon and let the air rush out. The
balloon will rocket along the line.

An idea was beginning to form in my brain. 'So how far can they go?' I asked.

'We've never found that out. We're always worried that they'll go so far that we'll never find them again.'

'And how big can you make one of the balloons?'

'Any size. That's not a problem.'

'Could you make one big enough to carry the space rocket?'

'We've already got one that big.'

'Sam, what exactly are you up to?' Sally asked.

'I'm just getting us out of here.'

I explained my plan to Sally and the alien. Bruto called his friends from their dragon shelters and explained the plan. They were happy to help because they thought Sally had saved them from the Sun Dragon.

'Sam, are you sure this is going to work?' Sally asked when we were sitting in the space rocket again. I'm not convinced that strapping the rocket to a big balloon is going to get us home.'

'It'll work. Trust me. We just need to get off the planet and then the space rocket can take over again. The gravity of the Sun will pull us back to Earth. It's a bit like starting a car.'

'But you've never done that either,' she said.

The aliens had finished blowing up the balloon and we were strapped into our seats. 'Goodbye, Bruto!'

'Goodbye, aliens!' they cheered and waved their boots in farewell. Time for another countdown. '5 . . . 4 . . . 3 . . . 2 . . .' and the computer screen flickered.

'Not again,' groaned Sally, 'not the evil scientist.'

'. . . 1'

As we took off into the Pluto sky, the figure on the screen became clearer but we must have been imagining it. That face! It couldn't have been Granny . . . *could* it?

Chapter 10

'Hello, you two!' Granny cried. 'Your mother says you missed your pancakes last night. Is it worth making you any breakfast this morning?'

'Granny!' I said to the face on the screen. 'How did you find us?'

'On that inter-netty thingy on Sally's computer. Where are you?' she asked.

'We've just left the planet Pluto and we're headed for Earth, Gran.'

'Did you bring me some rock?' she asked.

'Of course,' I said. 'I always do.'

'Good lad. What about breakfast?'

'What time is it on Earth?'

'Eight o'clock in the morning.'

Sally tapped the figures into her computer. 'We'll be landing at five minutes to nine, Gran,' she said. 'But we'll have to go straight to school to get Sam's project in on time. We'll have breakfast on the spaceship and then have a school dinner.'

Granny sucked hard on her gums. 'Ooooh! You poor things! I saw the school cook last night and she was looking very hard at some ponies in the field next to the school. I reckon it'll be horse-burgers and chips for school dinner today.'

'Same as usual,' I sighed. 'See you when we get back from school, Gran!'

She waved and her face vanished from the screen.

'There's only one problem,' Sally said. 'I'm not quite sure which of those bright dots in the sky is Earth!' She pointed through the window. 'If we aim for the wrong one we'll lose time. If only we had a telescope!'

'But we have, Sally!' I cried. 'I saw it in my comic this week! "Make your own telescope". All I need is your glasses!'

I pulled the comic from my pocket and looked at the instructions . . .

Roll Your Own Telescope

Why not spy on your friends?
Make this super snooper-scope and stick
your nose into other people's business.
(Or if you want to be really boring you
could use it to look at planets . . . or
find your way back to Earth from outer
space! Ho! Ho! Only joking!)
You need: an old pair of spectacles.
(Or why not pinch teacher's while she's
not looking? Ho! Ho! Only joking again!)

Instructions:
1 Take two lenses from a pair of old spectacles. (It's better with a thick lens and
a thin one but that means finding two pairs
of spectacles.)

2 Find two empty kitchen roll tubes
and slide one inside the other.

3 Put a lens in opposite
ends of the tube. You can
cut a slit in the tube to
hold the lens in place.

4 Look through your telescope
(with the thicker lens nearest
to your eye) and adjust the
length by sliding the tubes.

But here's a warning, readers! Never use
your telescope to look at the Sun! Wally
Warthog did and he blinded his silly self.
Now he has to go everywhere with a guide-
hog. Oh! Oh! No joking this time!

I took Sally's glasses from her fat little nose and I snapped them in two. 'My glasses! You broke my glasses!' she cried.

'They'll soon mend with a bit of chewing gum,' I told her. 'Now, here's the telescope . . . let's see what we can see!'

I looked out of the window and turned the telescope on the brightest planet.

I was looking back at Pluto.

Then I saw a reddish planet with lines on. I knew it had to be Mars. 'What are those lines on Mars?' I asked.

'They call them canals,' Sally said. 'Millions of years ago there was water on Mars and tiny organisms were found in Martian rock.'

'I'm glad I'm not taking that back for Gran,' I muttered and turned my telescope on a blue-green-white planet. 'Turn left a bit, Sally, and we're dead on course for Earth.'

Three-quarters of an hour later we were hurtling through the sky. I could see the seashore below us. With my telescope I could see a worried donkey on the beach looking up at us! 'Fire the rockets to slow us down!' I cried.

'We've no fool, you fuel!' she answered but I think she meant it the other way around. 'I've programmed the computer to land us on the beach where we left yesterday morning.'

'But we'll bury the town in sand if we hit it at this speed!' That was when I saw the handle . . .

IN CASE OF EMERGENCY
PULL THIS HANDLE →
PENALTY FOR IMPROPER USE £50

I pulled it. Suddenly a parachute snapped out from the rocket and slowed our sand-splattering drop. 'Too late!' Sally cried. 'We'll still break up when we hit that beach.'

It was sad really. We'd travelled half way round the world then half way round the solar system just to end up buried on the beach. I held on tightly to the arms of my seat and waited for the crunch.

'Ten seconds to impact!' Sally yelled. 'Goodbye, little brother. I'd like to tell you what a wonderful person you truly are . . . but I don't want my last words to be a lie! Three seconds . . . two . . . one . . .'

Chapter 11

Splash!!!!!

Splash????? We'd landed in *water*!

'That was lucky,' Sally said.

'What?' I asked.

'Landing in the sea.'

'How could drowning be better than crashing to Earth and being splattered? Since when has drowning been *lucky*, Sal?'

'We're not going to drown. These space capsules are designed to float.'

'So was the *Titanic*!' I muttered.

Which reminded me, if we had landed in the same place we left from yesterday then . . . where was the beach?

'Sal, where's the beach?'

'I'm glad you asked that,' she said. But I could see she wasn't. She wrinkled her fat little nose and frowned. I could almost hear the cogs whirring in her head as she tried to think of an explanation. 'Of course, it'll be the full moon.'

That's it, I thought, I'm out of here! I am stuck in a space capsule with a maniac who is talking about full moons. She'll turn into a werewolf next. Mind you, with those teeth and ears she's not far off.

'It's a spring tide.'

'Sally, how can it be a spring tide? It's summer.'

'A spring tide just means the sea water is higher than it normally is.'

'So do we just wait until a winter tide?' I asked.

'There's no such thing, you idiot.'

This was the time when I wanted Sally to tell me I was imagining everything. But I knew what was going to happen next. She produced yet another book from her backpack. I sometimes think she's got a complete library in there.

Ye Olde Sailing Booke by A. F. Ake.

Every schoolboy has heard the story of how Sir Francis Drake knew he had time to finish his game of bowls and still beat the Spanish Armada. But they must wonder how Drake knew. The answer is, he kept a lunar diary.

sounds more like a loony diary to me!

Follow these simple instructions and you can make one.

1 *Get a piece of black paper and cut out 29 circles — about 3 cm in diameter. Draw a grid that has seven columns down (one for each day of the week) and five rows across.*

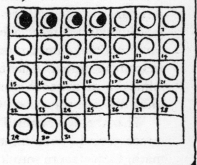

2 *Every night before you go to bed, look at the Moon.*

3 *Cut out the shape of the moon in aluminium
    foil and stick it on one of the circles.*

4 *By the end of the month you will have a complete lunar diary.*

'So where exactly did Francis Drake get aluminium foil from, Sally?'

'The point is that Drake knew he couldn't set off to sea until the tide had come in. So he finished his game of bowls first.'

'That's a brilliant excuse for not going to work. I must remember to tell Dad.'

Sally unfastened the hatch and looked out. She glanced across at the clock on the promenade then up to the school at the top of the hill. 'Look at the time! We need to get your project to school.'

'Sally, you may not have noticed this but we are in the middle of the sea.'

'No we're not, we are just about to be washed up on to the beach. The incoming tide has washed us on to the shore.'

I hate my sister all the time (it's my job) but I hate her most when she's right. We grabbed the back-pack and the computer and climbed out of the capsule. Where was the welcoming crowd? Where was the band? Where was our family to greet us? Why was that donkey looking at me like I'd just dropped out of the sky?

We had only a few minutes to get to school and deliver my project. I knew this time I was going to get a good mark. I knew there wasn't anyone who could have done a better project.

I knew that donkey shouldn't be able to take his skin off like that. I knew I was staring into the eyes of Master Minde.

Chapter 12

His face was as grey as the donkey skin he was stepping out from. 'Think you've beaten me, don't you, Spark?'

The clock on the promenade began to chime nine. 'Here's my project on "Earth, Moon and Stars", dead on time . . . sir!'

'Wipe that clever grin off your face, Spark, or I'll have you cleaning the school toilets for a week! Now let's get back to school for registration and I will mark this. If there are any mistakes . . . just one . . . then I'll have you picking up litter in the school playground on your hands and knees!'

'Thank you, sir,' I said. We set off to climb the narrow, steep streets from the sea front up to the school on the cliff top above. Master Minde's bat cloak flapped in the breeze and so did Sally's ears.

HAVE YOU TRIED THEM YET?
DO THEY WORK?

'I hope those experiments are all correct,' I whispered to her as we trailed behind the teacher.

'You tried them all for yourself,' she said.

Master Minde stormed into the classroom. 'Sit up straight, Class 5M! Put your hands on your heads!'

'Please, sir,' Kevin Crumble cried, 'I can't put my hands on my heads! I've only got one!'

'Only got one hand?' Minde snapped.

'No, sir. Only one head.'

'Shut up and stop breathing, you foolish boy,' the teacher ordered. He bent his head over my work and began to mark it. Then he turned a page and his black little eyes lit up! 'What is this nonsense about a jet made from a balloon?'

'The Plutonians showed us how to make that!' I said.

'There is no air on Pluto. How can you blow up a balloon without air?'

Sally tapped at her computer. 'The atmosphere of Pluto is methane gas. The Plutonians must breathe methane!'

'Aharrrrh! Sam, lad!' he cried . . . and he sounded just like Captain Jolly Roger who owned the ship. 'Unless you try it with *air* then the thing is just *mush*. Think you're a Bright Spark! Hah! My dog's got brighter barks than you!' And he sounded just like the Inuit who'd frozen Sally in the igloo.

'What if I can prove the balloon jet works with air on Earth?' I asked.

'It won't! What mark shall I give you for this project? Five . . . four . . . three . . . two . . . one?' And he sounded just like the Russian space scientist. I began to suspect Master Minde (in disguises) may have been behind some of the problems we'd had on our journey! It was almost as if he *wanted* me to fail with my project!

When the teacher said, 'Three . . . two . . . one!' there was a ripping of sticky tape as Sally pulled the seal off the balloon she'd been blowing up. 'Zero!' she cried. The balloon had been attached to the back of his chair. Master Minde rocketed into the air, through the roof of the school and up beyond the fluffy white clouds of the morning sky.

'I guess that's full marks, brother,' Sally said smugly. 'Don't thank me. Just buy me the biggest bar of chocolate in the universe.'

School was much more pleasant that day with Master Minde in orbit round the Earth. I went home to tea happier than ever . . . except that Sally was so-o-o-o-o-o pleased with herself.

When I got in the house Gran said, 'I've just been watching the news, Sam. Seems there's been a new comet spotted in the sky over our town. We'll be able to see it as soon as it gets dark.'

'Is it bright?'

'No, it's pretty stupid. It keeps shouting, 'I'm not a comet. I'm a teacher! Have you ever heard of such a thing?'

'No, Gran,' I said.

**Here is a list of the science experiments in this book.
Have you tried them all for yourself?**

If you have enjoyed this Sparks family adventure, why not try the others in the series?

Book Two: Chop and Change, 0 571 19369 2
Book Three: Shock Tactics, 0 571 19370 6
Book Four: Bat and Bell, 0 571 19371 4

These books are available from all good booksellers.
For further information please contact:

The Children's Marketing Department
Faber and Faber
3 Queen Square
London WC1N 3AU

Science Notes

Science Notes

Science Notes

Science Notes

ASTEROID
BELT

Science Notes

Science Notes

Science Notes

Science Notes